MY TEDDY BEAR

AT HOME

Teddy Bear is waiting for his friends to arrive.

They have promised to come and visit today.

Teddy hopes that they remember that it is a

rather important day for a little bear. He is

very excited, perhaps he will even get some

presents.

But first Teddy must tidy his room. His clothes are scattered all over the floor. One by one, he picks them up and puts them in the wardrobe. Oh dear, Teddy Bear has lost his socks. "There they are behind the clock," laughs his friend the Clown, who has just arrived with Little Wooden Duck. "Can we help?," they ask.

Little Wooden Duck helps Rag Rabbit make Teddy Bear's bed. He has found some clean sheets and a blanket in the cupboard. Making the bed is very hard work. At last it is done, except there is a funny bump right in the middle! What is it? Wooden Duck suddenly remembers, they have left the pillow under the sheets and will have to start all over again!

Wooden Doll is downstairs sweeping the floor with a brush. There are lots of crumbs under the table where she finds Teddy Bear's watch. He is always losing his things. Though he is very pleased that she has found it, he is also beginning to feel disappointed. Nobody has remembered that today is a special day.

At last his friends have helped him tidy up the house. Picking up a duster he begins to polish the mirror and dust the shelves. He has to stretch up high to reach them and he nearly knocks the goldfish out of its bowl. There are lots of ornaments to dust and he thinks he will never finish.

Elephant is helping by watering a large plant.

It's very thirsty. The plant has not been

watered for a long time, so Elephant uses his

long trunk to do the job. But while all of this

activity is going on, Wooden Doll and Clown

have prepared a surprise for Teddy.

Happy Birthday Teddy! The toys have just been helping to tidy up. They all came to arrange Teddy Bear's surprise party with balloons and streamers, and a magnificent cake. Teddy Bear is so happy. His friends didn't forget after all.

There are lots of dirty dishes to wash before the toys can play games. Teddy Bear washes all of the bowls and spoons, and his friends dry the dishes, ready to put away. Wooden Doll is very busy, making sure they all do their jobs properly.

Now that the kitchen is tidied and all the tea things cleared away, they all go up to the nursery. Teddy Bear rides his new rocking horse which he has named 'Picnic'. After they have played some games together it is time for his friends to go home. It has been a lovely day.

Teddy Bear enjoyed himself so much. He

thought everybody had forgotten it was his

birthday, it turned out to be the best ever. He

got a new tennis racket, a ball, and a shining

new yacht, as the day ended he was planning

his next adventure when he and his friends

would take the yacht out to the shallow

boating lake in the park.